ESTHER

A MODERN TALE OF LOVE AND INTEGRITY

WOMEN OF THE BIBLE FICTION
BOOK 2

KAYLA LOWE

Want a free book? Sign up to my newsletter to get my award-winning book for free! www.authorkaylalowe.com

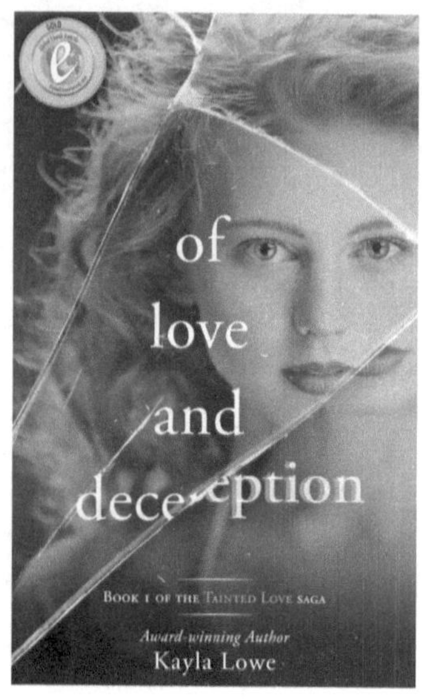

MORE OF MY BOOKS

Series

Charms of the Chaste Court

A Courtship in Covent Garden
Whispers in Westminster
Romance in Regent's Park
Serenade on Strand Street
Treasure in Tower Bridge

Sweet Honey by the Sea

The Beekeeper's Secret (Book 1)
A Royal Honeycomb (Book 2)
Bees in Blossom (Book 3)
Honeyed Kisses (Book 4)
Blooming Forever (Book 5)

Strawberry Beach Series

Beachside Lessons (Book 1)
Beachside Lessons (Book 2)
Beachside Lessons (Book 3)

Panama City Beach Series

Sun-Kissed Secrets (Book 1)
Sun-Kissed Secrets (Book 2)
Sun-Kissed Secrets (Book 3)

The Tainted Love Saga

Of Love and Deception (Book 1)
Of Love and Family (Book 2)
Of Love and Violence (Book 3)
Of Love and Abuse(Book 4)
Of Love and Crime (Book 5)
Of Love and Addiction (Book 6)
Of Love and Redemption (Book 7)

<u>Standalones</u>

Maiden's Blush

<u>Poetry</u>

Phantom Poetry
Lost and Found

CHAPTER 1

Esther's heels clicked against the polished marble floor of the sleek office tower as she strode towards the executive conference room, her thoughts a swirling tempest of ambition and apprehension. The weight of responsibility hung heavily upon her shoulders, a mantle she had willingly donned in her ascent through the corporate ranks. Yet, beneath the veneer of professionalism, the echoes of her humble beginnings lingered, a constant reminder of the delicate balance she sought to maintain between her burgeoning career and the unshakable bonds of family.

As she stepped into the conference room, the floor-to-ceiling windows offered a breathtaking panorama of the bustling metropolis below, a veritable labyrinth of hopes and dreams etched in steel and glass. Esther's gaze drifted to the horizon, where the sun's rays danced upon the distant rooftops, casting an ethereal glow that seemed to whisper of untold possibilities. She drew a steadying breath, steeling herself for the challenges that lay ahead, knowing that each decision she made would ripple through the lives of those she held dear.

Across town, in the hallowed halls of City Hall, Mayor Xander Harrison stood before a sea of eager faces, his charismatic presence commanding the attention of all who gathered. His voice, rich with authority and tinged with an undercurrent of empathy, resounded through the crowded chamber as he unveiled his latest initiative.

"My fellow citizens," he began, his piercing blue eyes sweeping over the assembled throng. "Today, we embark upon a journey that will reshape the very fabric of our beloved city. In our search for a new spokesperson, we seek not merely a voice, but a beacon of hope and inspiration. Together, we shall forge a path towards a brighter future, where every voice is heard, and every dream is within reach."

As the mayor's words washed over the captivated audience, a palpable energy surged through the room, igniting a spark of excitement and anticipation. The city's elite, resplendent in their tailored suits and designer gowns, exchanged knowing glances and hushed whispers, each vying for a piece of the limelight that would inevitably follow this momentous declaration.

Esther, lost in thought as she gazed out at the city below, felt a flicker of unease deep within her soul. She couldn't shake the feeling that her carefully constructed world was about to be upended, that the delicate equilibrium she had fought so hard to maintain was teetering on the brink of chaos. And yet, a small voice within her whispered that perhaps this was the very opportunity she had been seeking, a chance to make a difference, to leave an indelible mark upon the tapestry of her beloved city.

With a heavy sigh, Esther turned from the

window, her resolve hardening with each passing moment.

A sharp knock at her office door jolted Esther from her reverie. She smoothed the fabric of her skirt, a subtle armor against the unexpected, and called out, "Come in."

The door swung open, revealing the towering figure of her supervisor, Mr. Jameson. His usually stoic features were alight with an inscrutable emotion as he strode toward her desk, a crisp envelope clutched in his hand.

"Esther," he began, his voice a mix of incredulity and admiration, "I have some news that may come as a surprise to you." He paused, as if searching for the right words. "Mayor Harrison's office has personally requested your participation in the selection process for the new mayoral spokesperson."

The words hung in the air, their weight palpable. Esther's mind raced, trying to comprehend the implications of this unexpected development. She had always prided herself on her dedication to her work, her unwavering commitment to excellence, but this? This was beyond anything she had ever imagined.

"I...I don't know what to say," she managed, her voice barely above a whisper. "Why me?"

Mr. Jameson's lips curved into a wry smile. "Why not you, Esther? You've proven yourself time and again, both in your work and in your character. The mayor's office recognizes that, and they believe you have the potential to be an exceptional spokesperson for our city."

Esther's thoughts turned to her family, to the sacrifices they had made to support her dreams. She thought of the countless hours she had spent honing her skills, pushing herself to be better, to make a difference. And now, here was an opportunity to do just that, to step onto a larger stage and be a voice for change.

But even as excitement coursed through her veins, Esther couldn't shake the nagging doubts that crept into the corners of her mind. Was she truly ready for such a monumental responsibility? Could she bear the weight of an entire city's hopes and dreams upon her shoulders?

As if sensing her inner turmoil, Mr. Jameson leaned forward, his eyes locking with hers. "Esther, I know this is a lot to take in. But I also know that you have the strength, the intelligence, and the compassion to excel in this role. The decision is yours, but I have no doubt that you would make an extraordinary spokesperson for our city."

With those words, he placed the envelope on her desk and quietly took his leave, the door clicking shut behind him. Esther stared at the innocuous piece of paper, her heart pounding in her chest. She knew that the contents of that envelope held the power to change the course of her life, to set her on a path she had never dared to dream of.

And as she reached out with trembling fingers to grasp the envelope, Esther felt a surge of determination wash over her. Come what may, she would face this challenge with the same tenacity and grace that had brought her this far. For in this moment, she knew with unshakable certainty that her journey was only just beginning.

CHAPTER 2

Esther entered the grand hall, her modest heels clicking on the gleaming marble floor. The vaulted ceiling arched overhead, adorned with gilded frescoes that seemed to whisper tales of glory and ambition. Around her, the other contenders milled about in their designer suits and dresses, their chatter a cacophony of polished accents and well-rehearsed talking points.

As she made her way to the registration table, Esther felt the weight of their appraising gazes upon her. The doubtful quirk of an eyebrow, the dismissive curl of a lip—their silent judgments were deafening. She knew what they saw when they looked at her: a woman from a humble background, an outsider daring to step into their hallowed halls of influence.

But Esther held her head high, refusing to let their skepticism deter her. She had not come this far, fought this hard, to be cowed by the trappings of privilege. Her strength came from within, from the unshakable conviction that she was meant for more than the narrow confines of expectation.

As the first challenge commenced, Esther listened intently to the moderator's instructions. The task was to develop a comprehensive plan to address the city's homelessness crisis, one that balanced compassion with practicality. While the other contenders rushed to grab the microphone, eager to tout their credentials and connections, Esther took a moment to collect her thoughts.

When it was her turn to speak, her voice rang out clear and steady. "The measure of a society is how it treats its most vulnerable members," she began, her words imbued with quiet passion. "We must approach this issue not just with resources, but with empathy and understanding."

As she outlined her proposal, Esther's keen intellect shone through. She spoke of innovative housing solutions, job training programs, and partnerships with local organizations—ideas born not of lofty idealism, but of a deep understanding of the community's needs. Her calm demeanor never wavered, even as the other contenders peppered her with questions meant to trip her up.

From the corner of her eye, Esther noticed a few of the city's key influencers leaning forward in their seats, their interest piqued. She felt a flicker of satisfaction, knowing that her words were hitting their mark.

As the challenge drew to a close, Esther offered a silent prayer of thanks. She knew that this was only the beginning, that there were more trials to come. But in that moment, standing tall amidst the glittering trappings of power, she felt a sense of purpose settle over her like a mantle.

There was a moment of silence, and then the auditorium erupted in a cacophony of applause and excited chatter as the competition results were announced. Esther stood on the stage, her heart pounding with a mixture of disbelief and elation. Against all odds, she had emerged victorious, earning the coveted role of the city's new spokesperson.

As the reality of her achievement sank in, Esther's thoughts raced with the implications. This was no mere title. It was a position of immense influence and responsibility. She would now have a direct line to the city's decision-makers, a platform to advocate for the causes she held dear.

Amidst the sea of congratulatory handshakes and flashbulbs, Esther caught sight of her family in the audience. Her mother's eyes shone with pride, while her father nodded with quiet approval. In that moment, Esther felt a surge of gratitude for the values they had instilled in her—the same values that had guided her through this grueling competition.

As the event wound down and the crowds began to disperse, Esther found herself approached by a well-dressed woman with a shrewd glint in her eye. "Congratulations, Ms. Rodriguez," the woman said, extending a manicured hand. "I'm Olivia Blackwell, the mayor's chief of staff. We have high expectations for you."

Esther met the woman's gaze steadily, sensing the unspoken challenge in her words. "I'm ready to get to work," she replied, her voice ringing with quiet conviction. "I believe we can make a real difference in this city."

As she stepped off the stage and into her new role, Esther felt a weight settle on her shoulders. She knew that the real work was just beginning, that there would be obstacles and opposition at every turn. But she also knew, with a faith that burned bright within her, that she was not alone in this fight.

With a deep breath and a silent prayer, Esther stepped forward into the political fray, ready to be a voice for the voiceless and a champion for the forgotten. Come what may, she would face it all with the strength and grace that had brought her to this moment.

CHAPTER 3

Gabriel Collins leaned back in his plush leather chair, a serpentine smile curling his lips as he surveyed the glittering cityscape below. The late afternoon sun glinted off steel and glass, casting sharp-edged shadows that mirrored the ruthless machinations of his mind. Power was an intoxicating elixir, and he had every intention of quenching his thirst.

His eyes narrowed, calculating, as his gaze settled on the sprawling neighborhood in the distance—Esther Rodriguez's community, where hard-working families eked out humble lives amidst faded dreams and quiet desperation. They were ripe for exploitation, their trusting nature a weakness he would wield like a finely honed blade.

"The Riverdale project," Gabriel mused aloud, his rich baritone echoing in the cavernous office. "Buying up that land for a fraction of its worth, displacing those unsuspecting residents...It's almost too easy."

His right-hand man, a shrewd attorney with a shark's predatory instincts, nodded in agreement. "And with Esther Rodriguez as the public face, we'll have the perfect scapegoat if anything goes south. Her connection to that community will be our shield."

Unbeknownst to them, Esther stood just outside the door, her hand frozen on the polished brass handle. The cruel words sliced through her like shards of betrayal, their callous laughter an unholy chorus that made her soul recoil.

She saw with painful clarity the web of deceit they had spun, her role as an unwitting pawn in their twisted game. The weight of responsibility settled heavily upon her shoulders, a mantle she had never sought but could not now cast aside.

As Gabriel and his cohort continued to scheme, weaving tendrils of greed and treachery that threatened to strangle the very heart of her beloved community, Esther closed her eyes, a silent prayer for guidance rising from the depths of her being. The path ahead was fraught with peril, but she knew with bone-deep certainty that she could not stand idly by while innocents suffered.

The die was cast, the battle lines drawn. Esther Rodriguez, the unlikely champion, would fight for the souls of the forgotten, even as the forces of avarice and duplicity arrayed themselves against her. In that moment of reckoning, she felt the stirrings of a courage she had never known, a fire that would not be quenched by the chill winds of adversity. The gauntlet had been thrown, and she would meet it head-on, armed only with the strength of her convictions and the unshakable belief that justice would prevail.

Esther's mind raced as she paced the length of her modest apartment, the weight of her newfound knowledge bearing down upon her like a physical force. The muted sounds of the city beyond her windows faded into insignificance, drowned out by the clamor of her own tumultuous thoughts. She paused before the small mirror that hung above her bureau, catching a glimpse of her reflection—a woman transformed, her once-bright eyes now shadowed with the burden of truth.

"What am I to do?" she whispered, her voice trembling with a mixture of fear and resolve. "If I speak out, I risk everything I've worked so hard to achieve. But if I remain silent, how many will suffer?"

The faces of her neighbors, her friends, her community swam before her mind's eye—hard-working, honest people whose only crime was to dream of a better life. They trusted her, looked to her as a beacon of hope in an often-unforgiving world. Could she betray that trust, that sacred bond, for the sake of her own comfort and security?

Esther's gaze drifted to the worn Bible that rested on her nightstand, its pages well-thumbed and marked with the passage of time. She reached for it, seeking solace in its ancient wisdom, and found herself drawn to the story of Esther, the biblical queen who risked everything to save her people. The parallels were not lost on her, and she felt a strange kinship with her namesake, a woman called to stand against the forces of oppression and injustice.

As she read, a sense of peace began to settle

over her, the chaos of her thoughts giving way to a quiet certainty. She knew, with a clarity that surpassed mere understanding, that she could not turn a blind eye to Gabriel's machinations. To do so would be to betray everything she held dear, everything she believed in.

Esther closed the Bible, her decision made. She would confront Gabriel, would expose his schemes for the cruel and callous manipulations they were. She would be a voice for the voiceless, a champion for those who had no one else to fight for them. And though the road ahead was uncertain, though the price she might pay was high, she knew that she could face it with her head held high, secure in the knowledge that she was doing what was right.

With a deep breath, Esther squared her shoulders and prepared to face the battles to come. She was Esther Rodriguez, a woman of faith, of courage, of conviction. And she would not be moved.

CHAPTER 4

The grand ballroom sparkled with the glitter of the city's elite, crystal chandeliers casting a warm glow upon the sea of designer gowns and tailored suits. Esther stood at the periphery, her simple yet elegant black dress a stark contrast to the opulence surrounding her. She felt the weight of curious gazes upon her, whispers of speculation dancing through the air like a discordant melody.

As Mayor Harrison ascended the stage, his presence commanded the room's attention. His words wove a tapestry of promise and progress, each carefully chosen phrase designed to inspire and uplift. With a flourish, he gestured towards Esther, beckoning her to join him in the spotlight.

Esther's heart raced as she stepped forward, acutely aware of the significance of this moment.

She knew that with influence came responsibility, a burden she was both eager and apprehensive to bear. As she took her place beside the mayor, she caught sight of Gabriel Collins, his piercing blue eyes fixed upon her with an intensity that sent a chill down her spine.

Gabriel moved through the crowd with the grace of a panther, his charm as potent as it was insidious. He leaned in close to the mayor, his words a poisonous whisper. "Are you certain about her, Xander? A relative unknown, thrust into such a crucial role...It's a gamble that could cost you dearly."

The mayor's brow furrowed, a flicker of doubt passing across his features. But as he turned to face Esther, her unwavering gaze and quiet strength seemed to dispel the shadows Gabriel had cast. "I have faith in Esther's abilities," he declared, his voice carrying across the room. "She represents the best of our city—resilience, compassion, and an unwavering commitment to justice."

As applause filled the air, Esther felt a surge of gratitude mingled with trepidation. She knew that Gabriel's words were but the first salvo in a battle that would test her resolve and integrity. But in that moment, standing before the city's most influential figures, she vowed to herself that she would not falter, that she would fight for what was right, no matter the cost.

The banquet continued, a whirlwind of introductions and conversations that left Esther's mind reeling. She navigated the treacherous waters of high society with a mix of grace and determination, forging alliances and earning respect with each measured word and genuine smile. Yet always, at the edge of her consciousness, lurked the specter of Gabriel's malice, a reminder that her path forward would be fraught with challenges and adversaries.

As the evening drew to a close, Esther found herself alone on the balcony, the city's twinkling lights stretched out before her like a canvas of possibility. She breathed deeply, the cool night air a balm to her racing thoughts. In the distance, a church bell tolled, its solemn notes a reminder of the faith that had always guided her steps. With a whispered prayer, Esther steeled herself for the trials to come, knowing that with God's grace and her own unwavering resolve, she would emerge victorious, a beacon of hope for the city she loved.

Esther's hands trembled as she lifted the delicate teacup to her lips, the warmth of the ceramic a fleeting comfort against the chill that had settled in her bones. Across the table, Manny's eyes, usually filled with mirth and kindness, now held a somber intensity that made her heart clench. The bustling noise of the café faded into the background as Esther leaned forward, her voice barely above a whisper. "Manny, I don't know what to do. Gabriel's influence runs deeper than I ever imagined."

Manny reached across the table, his calloused hand enveloping hers in a gesture of support. "Esther, you can't let him win. His plans...they'll tear our community apart. The people, the families we've grown up with, they'll be the ones to suffer." His words hung heavy in the air, a weight that settled on Esther's shoulders like a mantle of responsibility.

She closed her eyes, images of the neighborhood she loved flashing through her mind. The laughter of children playing in the streets, the smell of fresh bread wafting from the bakery, the sense of belonging that had always been her anchor. To lose that, to see it shattered by Gabriel's machinations...the thought was unbearable.

Opening her eyes, Esther met Manny's gaze, a flicker of determination sparking to life within her. "What can I do, Manny? How do I stop him?"

Manny's grip tightened, his voice urgent. "You have to fight, Esther. Use your position, your influence. Rally the people behind you. Show them the truth of Gabriel's intentions." He paused, his expression softening. "You've always been the strongest of us, the one who never backs down from a challenge. This is your moment, your calling."

Esther's mind raced, the enormity of the task before her threatening to overwhelm her. But as she looked into Manny's eyes, saw the faith and trust reflected there, she felt a sense of calm wash over her. This was her path, her purpose. She had been placed in this position for a reason, and she would not shy away from it.

With a deep breath, Esther straightened her shoulders, a newfound resolve settling into her very bones. "I'll do it, Manny. I'll fight for our community, for what's right. No matter what it takes."

Manny's smile was a beacon of hope, a reminder that she was not alone in this battle. "I know you will, Esther. And we'll be right there with you, every step of the way."

As they sat in the quiet of the café, the weight of their shared purpose a tangible presence between them, Esther felt a whisper of the divine, a sense that God's hand was guiding her steps. She closed her eyes once more, a silent prayer falling from her lips. With faith as her shield and love as her sword, she would face the trials ahead, knowing that in the end, truth and justice would prevail.

CHAPTER 5

As the morning light filtered through the high-rise windows, casting stark shadows across the polished marble floor, Esther hurried through the quiet hallway towards Mayor Harrison's office. The echo of her heels betrayed a hint of urgency beneath her composed exterior. She clutched a folder filled with meticulously prepared proposals, each page a testament to her unwavering commitment to the city's most vulnerable.

With a steadying breath, Esther raised her hand to knock, only to hesitate as a flicker of doubt crossed her mind. Was she truly ready to navigate the labyrinthine world of politics? The weight of responsibility pressed upon her shoulders, a reminder of the lives that hung in the balance. No, she thought, squaring her shoulders. There was no turning back now. The people needed her.

Mayor Harrison greeted her with a warm smile, his eyes crinkling at the corners. "Esther! Come in, please. It's always a pleasure to see you."

Esther returned the smile, hoping it masked the trepidation that gnawed at her. "Thank you for making time to meet with me, Mayor Harrison. I know your schedule must be incredibly busy."

"Nonsense. Your work is a priority for this city." The mayor gestured for her to take a seat, leaning forward with an attentive gaze. "Tell me, what brings you here today?"

As Esther delved into her proposals, passion imbued her every word. "These reforms are crucial, sir. They will provide a safety net for our most vulnerable citizens—the elderly, the impoverished, the marginalized. We have a moral obligation to ensure their well-being."

Mayor Harrison nodded thoughtfully, thumbing through the pages. "Impressive, as always. But tell me, Esther—have you considered the political ramifications? Change, even necessary change, can ruffle feathers."

A flicker of uncertainty crossed Esther's face. She had anticipated resistance, but the mayor's words carried an ominous undertone. "I understand the risks," she said carefully. "But surely the welfare of our citizens should be our utmost priority?"

Unbeknownst to them both, Gabriel Collins lurked in the shadows of his own machinations. A ruthless puppeteer, he pulled strings from afar, weaving a web of deceit and corruption that threatened to ensnare Esther. With calculated precision, he sowed seeds of doubt among the city's elite, whispers of Esther's alleged involvement in unsavory dealings.

As the meeting drew to a close, Esther felt a glimmer of hope. The mayor's support, while not yet guaranteed, seemed within reach. She stepped out into the hallway, her heart a little lighter, only to be met by a sea of reporters. Cameras flashed, voices clamored, and accusatory questions filled the air.

"Ms. Rodriguez! Can you comment on the allegations of corruption within your office?"

"Is it true that you've been funneling city funds into personal projects?"

Esther froze, her mind reeling. How had they found out? No, she realized with a sinking feeling. There was nothing to find out. These were baseless rumors, carefully crafted to undermine her credibility.

With a deep breath, she faced the cameras, her voice steady. "These allegations are completely false and unfounded. I have always acted with integrity and in the best interests of this city. I will not be deterred from my mission to protect our most vulnerable citizens."

As she made her way through the throng of reporters, head held high, Esther couldn't shake the feeling that this was only the beginning. Someone powerful was working against her, and she would need all her strength and resolve to weather the coming storm. But for now, she took solace in the knowledge that she had done what was right. The rest would have to unfold as the divine saw fit.

The gentle chime of the café door drew Esther's attention from the swirling chaos of her thoughts. She looked up to see Manny, his brow furrowed with concern as he approached her table nestled in the back corner. The familiar scent of freshly brewed coffee and warm pastries enveloped her, a momentary respite from the storm brewing outside.

"Esther," Manny began, his voice low and urgent as he slid into the seat across from her. "I've been hearing things around town. People are talking, and it's not good."

She sighed, her fingers tightening around the warm ceramic mug. "I know, Manny. The rumors, the accusations...it's all part of Gabriel's plan to discredit me."

Manny leaned forward, his dark eyes searching hers. "It's more than that, Esther. He's not just trying to discredit you He's trying to destroy you. If you don't act soon, it might be too late."

A heavy silence settled between them, the weight of his words hanging in the air like a gathering storm cloud. Esther's mind raced, the gravity of her situation sinking in. She had always known that standing up for what was right would come at a cost, but she had never imagined the price would be so high.

"What can I do, Manny?" she asked, her voice barely above a whisper. "Gabriel has all the power, all the connections. I'm just one person trying to make a difference."

Manny reached across the table, his hand

covering hers in a gesture of comfort and support. "You're not alone, Esther. You have people who believe in you, who stand with you. But you need to make a bold move, something that will expose Gabriel for who he really is."

Esther's mind whirled with possibilities, each one more daunting than the last. She knew Manny was right, but the thought of confronting Gabriel head-on filled her with a sense of trepidation. She had seen firsthand the depths of his cruelty, the lengths he would go to maintain his grip on power.

"I don't know if I have the strength," she confessed, her voice trembling. "What if I fail? What if he wins?"

Manny squeezed her hand, his gaze unwavering. "You are stronger than you know, Esther. God has given you a spirit of courage and righteousness. Trust in His plan, and He will guide your path."

As she looked into Manny's eyes, Esther felt a flicker of hope ignite within her. Maybe she couldn't do this alone, but she wasn't alone. She had her faith, her friends, and the knowledge that she was fighting for something greater than herself.

With a deep breath, she nodded, a newfound

determination settling over her. "Okay," she said, her voice steady. "I'll do it. I'll find a way to expose Gabriel and bring the truth to light."

Manny smiled, pride shining in his eyes. "That's the Esther I know. Remember, no matter what happens, you have people who love you and believe in you. You're not in this fight alone."

As they rose from the table, Esther felt a sense of purpose wash over her. The road ahead would be difficult, but she knew in her heart that it was the right one. With a silent prayer for strength and guidance, she stepped out into the sunlit street, ready to face whatever challenges lay ahead.

CHAPTER 6

Esther took a deep breath as she stepped into the dimly lit coffee shop, her eyes scanning the room for familiar faces. She spotted two of her most trusted confidants—Maria, a sharp-minded journalist, and John, a seasoned city administrator —already seated at a corner table, their expressions somber yet determined.

As she made her way towards them, Esther's mind raced with the gravity of the situation at hand. Gabriel's corruption ran deep, like a cancer spreading through the city's veins, and she knew that exposing his misdeeds would be no small feat. But Esther also knew that she could not stand idly by while injustice prevailed.

"Thank you both for coming," Esther said

quietly as she slid into the booth beside Maria. "I know the risks you're taking by being here."

Maria reached out and squeezed Esther's hand reassuringly. "We've got your back, Esther. Gabriel's reign of corruption ends now."

John nodded in agreement, his weathered face etched with resolve. "I've seen too many good people fall victim to his schemes. It's time we take a stand."

As they huddled together, voices low and urgent, Esther felt a flicker of hope amidst the darkness. With Maria's investigative prowess and John's insider knowledge, they began to piece together the puzzle of Gabriel's misdeeds, gathering evidence and testimonies that would expose his true nature to the world.

But even as they worked tirelessly, Gabriel was already several steps ahead, weaving a web of deceit that threatened to ensnare them all. In the gleaming towers of his corporate empire, he pored over falsified financial reports with a cold, calculated precision, his lips curling into a smirk as he imagined the downfall of his enemies.

"Esther Rodriguez thinks she can outmaneuver me," Gabriel mused to himself, his fingers drumming against the polished mahogany of his desk.

"But she has no idea who she's dealing with. By the time I'm through with her, her precious reputation will be in tatters."

With a few keystrokes and a well-placed phone call, Gabriel set his plan in motion, manipulating the numbers and pulling the strings of his puppet media outlets. He knew that the court of public opinion could be swayed with the right spin, and he was a master of the game.

As the days passed, Esther found herself increasingly under fire, her every move scrutinized and twisted by Gabriel's machinations. Whispers of scandal and impropriety followed her like a shadow, casting doubt on her integrity and competence.

Yet even in her darkest moments, Esther clung to her faith, drawing strength from the knowledge that truth and justice would ultimately prevail. She refused to let Gabriel's lies define her, instead redoubling her efforts to gather the evidence that would bring him to his knees.

In the quiet of her office, Esther bowed her head in prayer, seeking guidance and resolve from a higher power. "Lord, give me the strength to see this through," she whispered, her voice trembling with emotion. "Help me to be a light in this darkness, to stand firm in the face of adversity."

And as she raised her eyes, Esther knew that no matter what trials lay ahead, she would not falter in her pursuit of righteousness. For in the end, it was not just her own reputation at stake, but the very soul of the city itself.

Esther stood before the sea of reporters, their cameras flashing like a thousand stars in the night sky. The weight of the moment pressed upon her, but she refused to let it crush her spirit. With a deep breath, she stepped up to the podium, her eyes scanning the crowd before locking onto the lens of the central camera.

"Citizens of our beloved city," she began, her voice steady and clear, "I come before you today with a heavy heart, but also with an unwavering commitment to the truth. For too long, we have been deceived by those who seek to further their own interests at the expense of the common good. Today, I stand here to expose the corruption that has taken root in the very heart of our community."

As she spoke, Esther could feel the energy in the room shift, the murmurs of the reporters giving way to a hushed anticipation. She knew that her words would be met with skepticism, that Gabriel's influence ran deep, but she pressed on, undeterred.

"Gabriel Collins, a man many of you know and trust, has been manipulating our city's finances for his own gain," she revealed, her voice ringing with conviction. "He has used his position to siphon funds, to make deals that benefit only himself and his allies, all while painting himself as a savior and me as a villain."

The room erupted in a flurry of questions, reporters clamoring for more information, but Esther held up a hand, silencing them with her quiet authority. "I have evidence," she declared, "documents and testimony from brave individuals who have come forward to expose the truth. I will not rest until justice is served, until our city is free from the grip of those who would use their power to oppress and exploit."

As she spoke, Esther could feel the weight of Gabriel's gaze upon her, his eyes boring into her from the back of the room. She met his stare unflinchingly, her own eyes alight with the fire of righteousness. In that moment, she knew that she had struck a blow against his empire of lies, that the truth would be her sword and her shield in the battles to come.

"I ask you, the people of this city, to stand with me," she implored, her voice ringing with passion. "Together, we can build a future founded on integrity, compassion, and justice. We can be a light in the darkness, a beacon of hope for all who have been oppressed by the machinations of the powerful."

As the press conference drew to a close, Esther stepped back from the podium, her heart racing with a mixture of fear and exhilaration. She knew that the road ahead would be long and treacherous, that Gabriel would not surrender his power without a fight. But in that moment, as she looked out over the sea of faces, she saw something that gave her hope: the glimmer of recognition, the spark of belief in the eyes of those who had heard her words.

And as she walked from the stage, Esther knew that whatever trials lay ahead, she would face them with the strength of her convictions and the support of those who believed in the power of truth to triumph over darkness.

CHAPTER 7

The television screens across the city flickered with Esther's impassioned plea, her words reverberating through the streets and into the hearts of the citizens. Within moments, a chorus of voices rose in unison, demanding truth and accountability from those entrusted with the city's welfare. The media, ever-vigilant, seized upon the story, their cameras and microphones thrust towards the mayor's office, seeking a response to the allegations that threatened to unravel the very fabric of their society.

Esther strode through the hallowed halls of the municipal building, her footsteps echoing with the weight of her purpose. In her hands, she clutched the evidence that would bring Gabriel's corrupt empire crashing down, the truth that had been hidden for far too long. She thought of the countless lives that had been shattered by his greed and deceit, the dreams that had been crushed beneath the wheels of his ambition. But now, armed with the proof of his misdeeds, she would ensure that justice would prevail.

As she approached Mayor Harrison's office, Esther's heart raced with a mixture of anticipation and trepidation. She knew that the path ahead would not be easy, that Gabriel's influence ran deep and wide. But she also knew that she could not stand idly by while evil triumphed. With a deep breath, she pushed open the door and stepped inside.

Mayor Harrison looked up from his desk, his eyes widening as he took in Esther's determined expression. "Esther, what brings you here?" he asked, his voice tinged with surprise and concern.

Esther placed the file on his desk, her hands trembling slightly as she did so. "Mayor Harrison, I have evidence that Gabriel Collins has been using his position to further his own interests at the expense of the city and its people. He must be stopped before it's too late."

The mayor leaned back in his chair, his brow furrowed as he considered her words. "These are serious allegations, Esther. I hope you understand the gravity of what you're suggesting."

"I do," she replied, her voice steady and clear. "But I also understand the cost of remaining silent. We have a duty to the people of this city, to ensure that their trust is not betrayed by those who seek to abuse it."

Mayor Harrison sighed heavily, the weight of his office bearing down upon him. He had known Gabriel for years, had counted him among his closest allies. But as he looked into Esther's eyes, he saw the truth that he had long suspected but had been too afraid to confront.

With a nod, he reached for the file, his fingers tracing the edges of the pages that held the key to their city's future. "Let me see what you have," he said, his voice heavy with resignation. "And may God help us all."

As Esther watched him begin to read, she felt a flicker of hope rising within her. She knew that the road ahead would be long and difficult, that Gabriel would not go down without a fight. But she also knew that she was not alone, that there were others who shared her commitment to justice and truth. Together, they would build a brighter future for their city, one in which corruption and greed had no place.

And as she stood there in the mayor's office, the sunlight streaming through the windows and casting a warm glow upon the room, Esther felt a sense of peace wash over her. She had done what was right, had spoken truth to power, and now, the rest was in God's hands. Whatever the future held, she knew that she would face it with courage and faith, secure in the knowledge that she had fought the good fight and had emerged victorious.

Mayor Harrison's brow furrowed as he pored over the documents, the weight of Esther's revelations settling heavily upon his shoulders. The evidence was irrefutable, painting a damning picture of Gabriel's nefarious dealings and the insidious web of corruption that had ensnared their city. With each page, the enormity of the task before him grew clearer, the need for decisive action more pressing.

He rose from his desk, his steps measured as he approached the window overlooking the bustling metropolis. The city's skyline stretched before him, a testament to the hopes and dreams of its citizens, now tarnished by the shadow of Gabriel's misdeeds. In that moment, Xander knew that he could no longer remain silent, that the truth must be brought to light, no matter the cost.

With a heavy sigh, he turned to face Esther, his eyes hardened with resolve. "We must act swiftly," he declared, his voice tinged with a newfound determination. "The people deserve to know the truth, and Gabriel must be held accountable for his actions."

Together, they crafted a plan, a careful choreography of press conferences and public statements designed to expose Gabriel's corruption and rally the citizens to their cause. As the news broke, the city erupted in a maelstrom of outrage and disbelief, the once-untouchable executive now the target of scorn and condemnation.

In the days that followed, Gabriel's empire crumbled, his allies deserting him as the weight of his misdeeds became too great to bear. The authorities moved swiftly, arresting him and his accomplices, their once-powerful figures now reduced to mere shadows of their former selves.

As the dust settled, Mayor Harrison stood before the people, his voice a beacon of hope amidst the chaos. "Today, we have taken a stand against corruption and greed," he proclaimed, his words echoing through the streets. "We have shown that no one, no matter how powerful, is above the law. And together, we will build a brighter future for our city, one founded on the principles of justice, integrity, and compassion."

In the aftermath of Gabriel's downfall, the city began to heal, the wounds of corruption slowly mending as a new era dawned. And through it all, Esther and Mayor Harrison stood side by side, their partnership a testament to the power of faith and the indomitable spirit of those who fight for what is right.

As they looked out over the city, the sun setting behind the horizon, they knew that their work was far from over. But they also knew that they had taken the first steps towards a better tomorrow, and that with God's grace, they would continue to lead their people towards a future filled with hope and promise.

CHAPTER 8

Esther stood on the stage beside Mayor Harrison, a sense of vindication and relief washing over her as she gazed out at the sea of reporters and onlookers. The morning sunlight streamed through the windows of City Hall, casting a golden glow on the historic chamber. She took a deep breath, steadying herself as the mayor stepped up to the podium.

"Citizens of our great city," Mayor Harrison began, his voice resonating with authority and sincerity, "today marks a turning point in our history. The corruption that has plagued our government, embodied by the actions of Gabriel Collins, has been exposed and rooted out. Thanks to the bravery and integrity of one woman, Esther

Rodriguez, we can now begin the process of healing and rebuilding trust in our institutions."

Esther felt a lump form in her throat as the mayor spoke. She thought back to the long nights spent pouring over documents, connecting the dots of Gabriel's web of deceit. It had been a lonely and perilous journey, but her unwavering commitment to justice had sustained her. Now, as she stood in the light, she knew it had all been worth it.

Mayor Harrison turned to Esther, his blue eyes shining with admiration. "Ms. Rodriguez, your courage and dedication to the truth have been an inspiration to us all. In recognition of your vital role in uncovering this scandal, I would like to formally offer you a position as a key advisor in shaping our city's new policies. Your insight and moral compass will be invaluable as we work to prevent such abuses of power from ever happening again."

Esther's heart swelled with gratitude and purpose. She stepped forward, her voice clear and resolute. "Thank you, Mayor Harrison. I am honored to accept this responsibility. Together, we will rebuild our city on a foundation of transparency, accountability, and integrity. Let this be a message to all those who would seek to abuse their power for personal gain: the truth will always prevail."

As applause filled the chamber, Esther felt a sense of hope and determination surge within her. The road ahead would be long and challenging, but with the support of her community and the strength of her convictions, she knew they could create a brighter future for all. The light of truth had triumphed over the darkness of corruption, and a new era was dawning for the city she loved.

The sun-dappled streets of her childhood neighborhood welcomed Esther like a warm embrace as she stepped out of her car. The familiar scent of blooming jasmine and freshly cut grass mingled with the aroma of her mother's cooking wafting from the open windows of the modest family home. It was a scent that never failed to evoke memories of love, laughter, and the unwavering support that had shaped her into the woman she was today.

As she made her way up the well-worn path, the front door burst open, and a gaggle of nieces and nephews rushed out to greet her. "Aunt Esther! Aunt Esther!" they cried, their small arms encircling her waist and their bright eyes filled with adoration. Esther felt her heart swell with love as she bent down to return their embraces, the weight of the past few weeks momentarily lifted from her shoulders.

"Welcome home, mija," her mother said softly, appearing in the doorway with a proud smile. "We always knew you were destined for great things, but you've surpassed even our wildest dreams."

Esther felt tears prick the corners of her eyes as she stepped into her mother's waiting arms. The warmth of her embrace was a balm to her weary soul, a reminder that no matter how turbulent the world outside might be, she would always have a place of solace and unconditional love here.

As the family gathered around the dining table, the conversation flowed freely, punctuated by laughter and the clinking of dishes. Esther's father, a man of few words but endless wisdom, raised his glass in a toast. "To our Esther," he said, his voice thick with emotion, "a true hero who stood up for what was right, no matter the cost. You have brought honor to our family and to our community."

Esther felt a lump form in her throat as she looked around at the faces of those she loved most in the world. Their unwavering belief in her, their pride in her accomplishments, was a testament to the values they had instilled in her from a young age. Integrity, compassion, and the courage to stand up for what was right—these were the lessons she had learned at this very table.

As the evening wore on and the stars began to twinkle in the inky sky, Esther found herself sitting on the front porch swing, her mother's hand clasped tightly in her own. "I was so afraid," Esther confessed, her voice barely above a whisper. "Afraid that I wouldn't be strong enough, that I would let everyone down."

Her mother smiled softly, the lines around her eyes crinkling with understanding. "True strength, mija, comes not from an absence of fear, but from the courage to face it head-on. And that is exactly what you did. You stood tall in the face of adversity, and you emerged victorious. Never forget that."

Esther nodded, her heart filled with a renewed sense of purpose. She knew that the road ahead would be filled with challenges, but with the love and support of her family and community, she felt invincible. Together, they would build a city that valued truth, justice, and the inherent dignity of every human being. And Esther would be at the forefront of that change, a beacon of hope and integrity for all those who looked to her for guidance.

As the night drew to a close and Esther prepared to leave, her mother pressed a gentle kiss to her forehead. "Remember, mija," she whispered, "you are never alone. We are always with you, no matter where your path may lead."

With those words echoing in her heart, Esther stepped out into the night, ready to face whatever challenges lay ahead. She was Esther Rodriguez, a woman of courage, conviction, and unshakable integrity. And she would never stop fighting for what was right.

CHAPTER 9

Esther gazed out the large window of her new office in City Hall, the early morning light casting a golden hue across her pensive face. The weight of responsibility settled heavily on her shoulders, yet there was a quiet strength in her posture—a resilience forged through trials and tempered by faith.

She turned back to the stack of documents on her desk, each one representing a piece of the intricate puzzle she was determined to solve. The vulnerable populations of the city had suffered for too long under the shadow of corruption and neglect. It was time for change, and Esther knew she had been called for such a time as this.

With a steady hand, she began drafting the first of many reforms, her mind sharp and focused.

Each word was carefully chosen, each phrase crafted with purpose. She worked closely with trusted city officials, those who shared her vision of a just and transparent government. Together they pored over budgets, allocated resources, and established new programs to uplift the marginalized.

As the weeks turned into months, Esther watched as her tireless efforts began to bear fruit. Shelters were established for the homeless, job training programs launched for the unemployed, and stricter regulations put in place to hold those in power accountable. Slowly but surely, the city began to transform under her guidance.

In rare moments of quiet, Esther reflected on the path that had led her here. She thought back to her humble beginnings, the values instilled in her by a loving community. She remembered the challenges she had faced in the corporate world, the times when her integrity had been tested. Each experience had shaped her, molding her into the leader she was today.

And now, as she stood at the helm of a city on the brink of change, Esther realized that her journey had been one of divine purpose. She had been granted a platform, a voice to speak for those who had been silenced for too long. With each passing day, she grew more resolute in her mission, her faith an unshakable foundation amidst the turbulent tides of politics.

Esther's influence extended far beyond the walls of City Hall. Her name became synonymous with integrity and compassion, a beacon of hope for those who had lost faith in the system. Citizens who had once felt forgotten now looked to her as their champion, their voices joining together in a chorus of support.

Yet even as her star ascended, Esther remained grounded in her convictions. She knew that true change was not the work of one person alone, but the collective effort of a community united in purpose. She sought out the wisdom of elders, listened to the dreams of the youth, and wove their aspirations into the tapestry of her vision.

In the quietude of her office, late at night when the city slumbered, Esther would often pause to reflect on the weight of her role. She would kneel in prayer, seeking guidance and strength from a source greater than herself. It was in these moments of introspection that she found clarity, her path illuminated by the unwavering light of her faith.

As the years unfolded, the city blossomed under Esther's stewardship. The once-neglected neighborhoods now thrived with renewed vitality, their streets lined with flourishing businesses and vibrant community centers. The air hummed with a palpable sense of hope, a testament to the transformative power of compassionate leadership.

Esther's legacy was not measured in mere accolades or political victories, but in the lives she had touched, the destinies she had altered. She had become more than a leader. She was a catalyst for change, a conduit for the divine spark that resided within every human heart.

And as she stood at the precipice of a new chapter, her eyes fixed on the horizon of a brighter future, Esther knew that her journey was far from over. For as long as there were lives to be uplifted, wrongs to be righted, she would continue to serve, to lead with unwavering conviction and an abiding faith in the goodness of God.

EPILOGUE

The morning sun glinted off the polished brass plaque next to Esther's weathered door, proclaiming "Esther Rodriguez, Mayor." The words, though familiar after all these years, still filled her with a sense of wonder and gratitude. She stepped out onto the balcony overlooking the city square, her joints aching slightly with the effort. Below, the bustling marketplace hummed with activity, vendors hawking their wares as citizens went about their day under the watchful eyes of the new constabulary—men and women dedicated to fairness and the rule of law.

Esther's gaze drifted to the towering statue at the center of the square, a monumental figure of Justice, her scales held high. The sight brought a wistful smile to the old woman's face. The journey to this moment had been long and fraught with peril, a winding path that led from her humble beginnings to the halls of power and influence.

As if summoned by the thought, memories flooded Esther's mind—standing tall before hostile crowds, her voice unwavering as she called for reform, long nights hunched over legislation, wrestling with budgets and statutes, whispered threats and the cold press of fear against her heart as she stared down the barrel of a would-be assassin's gun. Each challenge, each trial endured had shaped her, molding her into the leader her city needed.

But it was the quieter moments, Esther mused, that had truly defined her. Late night conversations with her husband, his steadfast support a balm to her wearied soul. The flicker of pride in her mother's eyes as she watched her daughter take the oath of office. The tight embrace of a constituent, tears of gratitude dampening her shoulder. These intimate, profoundly human connections had fueled her, driving her ever onward.

A sudden commotion drew Esther's attention back to the present. In the square below, a child darted into the path of an oncoming cart, his mother's panicked scream piercing the air. But before tragedy could unfold, a young constable leapt forward, snatching the boy to safety with mere inches to spare. As the mother clutched her child close, sobbing with relief, the constable knelt to comfort them, his gentle words carrying on the breeze.

Esther felt her heart swell, a sudden thickness in her throat. This, she knew, was her true legacy - not the grand feats or public acclaim, but those small acts, those enduring sparks of human decency, kindled and nurtured through the power of example. And as she looked out over her city, radiant in the light of a new dawn, Esther knew with the warmth of certainty that while her part in the story might be drawing to a close, the torch would be carried forth, the work would continue, lifted higher by the next generation. With one last smile, Esther turned from the balcony and stepped inside, ready to face the day ahead.

The grand hall hummed with anticipation as Esther made her way to the stage, her steps measured, her head held high. The sea of faces before her blurred—old friends, new allies, even former adversaries, all united in this moment of tribute. As she ascended the podium, the room fell silent, every eye fixed upon her.

"Today," Esther began, her voice resonant with emotion, "we gather not to celebrate one person, but the indomitable spirit of a community. The courage we honor is not mine alone, but lives within each of you - the courage to stand tall in the face of injustice, to lift our voices for those who have been silenced, to fight for the dignity that is every person's birthright."

Her gaze swept the room, locking eyes with the young constable from the square, with the mother cradling her child. "The true measure of a life," she continued, "lies not in the accolades we garner, but in the seeds of compassion we plant, the ripples of change we set in motion with every choice to put another's needs before our own."

As the crowd erupted into applause, Esther felt a hand grasp hers—Mayor Harrison, her oldest friend and her staunchest ally. Their eyes met, a lifetime of shared struggles and triumphs passing between them. "You did it, Esther," her friend whispered, "you made a difference."

But Esther shook her head. "No," she corrected

gently, "*we* did it. Together. And that work is never finished." She squeezed her friend's hand. "But today...today we celebrate how far we've come. And tomorrow..." Her smile broadened, eyes sparkling with undimmed determination. "Tomorrow, we continue the journey."

As the crowd surged forward to embrace her, Esther closed her eyes, feeling the love, the gratitude, the shared hope wash over her, for she knew God would always look out for her people.

EXCERPT FROM RACHEL

Rachel wakes from sleep as the winter dawn light slants through her bedroom window. A vision of beauty and poise, she rises resiliently, as if invigorated by the new day with all its promise and possibilities.

She prepares mentally and physically for the important business event where she will network with the city's elite entrepreneurs. Glancing at her reflection, Rachel sees a polished, elegant woman, tall and graceful, whose outward appearance commands attention. She adorns herself in a designer outfit that exudes power and status. Secretly though, Rachel fears this facade masks the hidden insecurities lurking beneath the surface—the tremendous pressure to maintain her perfect, successful image at all costs.

Across town, Leah begins her day with quiet grace, inner goodness radiating from her like a serene glow. Where Rachel mesmerizes with magnetism and charisma, Leah captivates with calming compassion and keen intuition. Heading to work at the non-profit where she pours her heart into helping the underprivileged, Leah's simple, comfortable attire reflects her humble demeanor and gentle spirit.

As Rachel strides into her high-rise office, Leah slips behind the scenes at the organization she serves, both working in their own spheres. The contrasting sisters, each extraordinary in her own way, set about their divergent days.

Rachel reviews her marketing proposals with a critical eye, aiming for flawless campaigns to impress at the networking event. Her brilliant mind hums, strategizing how to outshine the competition. Yet a fleeting unease gnaws at her. Is this relentless ambition distancing her from what matters most? From family? From herself?

Miles from the glittering towers of commerce, Leah immerses herself in advocacy for vulnerable children, a light illuminating dark corners of injustice. She emanates empathy and understanding, a soothing presence for troubled souls. But in rare moments alone, doubt creeps in, an echo of her parents' disapproval. Why can't she command crowds like Rachel? Be the star, not the shadow?

The White sisters, bound by blood, remain worlds apart as they follow their true paths through life. Rachel ascends to dizzying corporate heights while Leah uplifts the downtrodden with selfless devotion. Each admirable, each incomplete without the other to lend balance and perspective. Their ultimate challenge lies in bridging the distance between them to forge an unbreakable bond transcending all measures of success.

***

Jacob Bennett stepped out of the sleek black car that had ferried him from the airport, his polished shoes making contact with the bustling city sidewalk. He paused for a moment, inhaling deeply as he surveyed the towering skyscrapers that stretched endlessly toward the heavens. The urban landscape hummed with an electric energy, a palpable current of ambition and opportunity that resonated deep within his entrepreneurial spirit.

As he strode purposefully toward his hotel, Jacob's thoughts wandered to the upcoming networking event that had drawn him to this metropolis. He had built a formidable reputation in the culinary world, his chain of upscale restaurants renowned for their innovative cuisine and impeccable service. Yet, he knew that complacency was the enemy of progress. To truly expand his empire, he needed to forge new connections, to immerse himself in the dynamic tapestry of the city's business elite.

A gentle breeze ruffled Jacob's carefully styled hair as he navigated the crowded streets, his mind already charting the course of his evening. He envisioned himself mingling effortlessly with the crème de la crème of the corporate world, his natural charisma and keen business acumen allowing him to forge valuable alliances. And yet, beneath the veneer of confidence, a flicker of uncertainty danced in his piercing blue eyes. Success had come at a price, demanding sacrifices that left him questioning the true meaning of fulfillment.

As he entered the opulent lobby of his hotel, Jacob's gaze fell upon a striking poster advertising the very event he had come to attend. The image of a woman, her face obscured but her presence commanding, caught his attention. There was something about her, an aura of strength and determination that resonated with his own drive. In that fleeting moment, Jacob felt an inexplicable pull, a sense that this mysterious figure held the key to a profound revelation.

With renewed purpose, Jacob made his way to his suite, his mind consumed by thoughts of the impending gathering. He knew that this event held the potential to shape the trajectory of his future, both professionally and personally. As he meticulously prepared for the evening, selecting an impeccably tailored suit and rehearsing his elevator pitch, Jacob couldn't shake the lingering image of the enigmatic woman from the poster. Little did he know that their paths were destined to intertwine, setting in motion a chain of events that would challenge everything he thought he knew about success, love, and the delicate balance between ambition and authenticity.

Get Rachel: A Modern Tale of Love and Sisterhood now!

ABOUT THE AUTHOR

Award-winning author Kayla Lowe writes women's fiction that explores complex themes with sensitivity and depth. Kayla's books delve into the intricacies of relationships, self-discovery, and resilience. From cozy love stories interspersed with a bit of faith to heartwarming tales of friendship and suspenseful novels of empowerment and heartbreak, her books illustrate the struggles specific to women.

When she's not churning out her next novel, you can find her with her feet in the sand and a book in her hand or curled up on the couch with her dogs.

Visit her website at www.authorkaylalowe.com.

ALSO BY KAYLA LOWE

<u>Series</u>

<u>Charms of the Chaste Court</u>

A Courtship in Covent Garden

Whispers in Westminster

Romance in Regent's Park

Serenade on Strand Street

Treasure in Tower Bridge

<u>Sweet Honey by the Sea</u>

<u>The Beekeeper's Secret (Book 1)</u>

<u>A Royal Honeycomb (Book 2)</u>

<u>Bees in Blossom (Book 3)</u>

<u>Honeyed Kisses (Book 4)</u>

<u>Blooming Forever (Book 5)</u>

<u>Strawberry Beach Series</u>

<u>Beachside Lessons (Book 1)</u>

<u>Beachside Lessons (Book 2)</u>

<u>Beachside Lessons (Book 3)</u>

Panama City Beach Series

Sun-Kissed Secrets (Book 1)

Sun-Kissed Secrets (Book 2)

Sun-Kissed Secrets (Book 3)

The Tainted Love Saga

Of Love and Deception (Book 1)

Of Love and Family (Book 2)

Of Love and Violence (Book 3)

Of Love and Abuse(Book 4)

Of Love and Crime (Book 5)

Of Love and Addiction (Book 6)

Of Love and Redemption (Book 7)

<u>Standalones</u>

Maiden's Blush

<u>Poetry</u>

Phantom Poetry

Lost and Found